everybody hates chris ™

Everybody Hates
Best Friends

everybody hates chris ™

Everybody Hates
Best
Friends

by Brian James

Simon Spotlight
New York   London   Toronto   Sydney

This book is a work of fiction. Any references to historical events, real people, or real locales are used fictitiously. Other names, characters, places, and incidents are the product of the author's imagination, and any resemblance to actual events or locales or persons, living or dead, is entirely coincidental.

Based on the TV series *Everybody Hates Chris*™ as seen on The CW.

SIMON SPOTLIGHT
An imprint of Simon & Schuster Children's Publishing Division
1230 Avenue of the Americas, New York, New York 10020
™ and © 2007 CBS Studios Inc. All Rights Reserved.
All rights reserved, including the right of reproduction in whole or in part in any form.
SIMON SPOTLIGHT and colophon are registered trademarks of Simon & Schuster, Inc.
Manufactured in the United States of America
First Edition 10 9 8 7 6 5 4 3 2 1
ISBN-13: 978-1-4169-3796-8
ISBN-10: 1-4169-3796-X
Library of Congress Catalog Card Number 2007933155

Chapter 1

There's something about Monday mornings that always stinks. It isn't just because Monday is garbage day on my block either. I don't know what it is for sure, but for some reason Mondays are the worst. Part of it has to do with school, a big part of it. After two days of sleeping and being lazy, my life goes right back to waking up early and dealing with tests and homework. For the most part, I can handle all of that. It's the bad luck that seems to always go along with Monday that I have trouble handling.

My string of extra-rotten Mondays started three weeks ago, when I missed the bus on the way to school. That didn't mean I got to stay home from school. I never get to stay home from school. The only thing missing the bus meant was that I had to race the bus five blocks to the next stop. The bus driver saw me waving for him to stop, but he just drove faster. And that was only the first bus! I live so far from my school that I have to take two buses to get there. Believe it or not, I missed the second one too.

It took me ten blocks to catch that one!

Two Mondays ago my report on the American Revolution was due. I spent all weekend working on it. I even spent the Friday before at the library reading about the fight for independence. I gave up *my* independence for three days to finish that report, only to leave it the kitchen table. I tried telling my teacher that it was done. I even said she could call my mom and ask her. But my teacher had heard that story used as an excuse too many times to believe me.

This past Monday was no different. Okay, so I didn't miss the bus and I didn't forget anything either. But my bad luck was still waiting for me at the start of first period. And it was getting meaner every week. It was like a neighborhood bully who starts out asking for your lunch money and ends up stealing your bike and your sneakers. It was clear to me the second I took my seat that this week my bad luck was going after everything I had.

It started when I dropped my pencil on the floor. I bent down in my chair to pick it up, and that's when I heard the tiny *rip*. My eyes popped wide open—I knew that sound right away. Every kid in the world who's ever split his pants before knows that sound. It was the sound of doom. My pants had split down the back!

I couldn't believe it. I checked around to see if anyone else had noticed. It didn't seem like anyone besides me had heard the rip. But no matter how quiet a noise it made, I knew that sooner or later, everyone would find out. Then my butt would be the butt of everyone's jokes for the rest of the week.

And believe me, the kids at Corleone Jr. High didn't need another reason to make fun of me. They seemed to have plenty of reasons already. This was going to make me the laughingstock of the school. I'd be more of an outcast than the weird kid who wears his clothes backward and calls all the teachers "Mom." I didn't want that!

So I spent all of history class trying to figure out how I was going to get out of this one. But I couldn't think of anything. And the longer I thought about it, the more I felt my jeans tearing wide open. Every time I moved an inch, I felt them rip a little wider. I stopped moving altogether, but it seemed like they still tore open a little more with each breath I took. Since I couldn't stop breathing, I had no choice but to let the worst happen.

By the time the bell rang, I could tell the backside of my jeans was flapping around like the flag outside on the flagpole. There was only one thing I could do: stay glued to my seat for as long as I could.

"Chris, aren't you going to your next class?" my teacher asked once the last kid had left. I glanced into the hallway, where kids were rushing by on their way to their next class. I could just imagine each and every one of them stopping in their tracks and pointing at my pants the second I stood up.

I looked back at my teacher and smiled.

I thought of something my dad always says whenever my mom is yelling at him that we are going to be late getting to where we need to go. "I'm just waiting until the traffic dies down," I said. Then I smiled again, trying to play it cool.

Playing it cool is something I've never been good at. I've tried many times, but I always fail. Last summer I tried to play it cool jumping off the high dive at the public swimming pool for the first time. I strutted my way out to the edge, slipped, and belly flopped smack dab on my face. Playing it cool hurt for two days that time. I had a funny feeling that playing it cool would hurt for a lot longer this time if the school bully, Joey Caruso, found out that I'd split my pants in half. So I was determined not to let him or anyone else find out, even if I had to sit in that seat until school was over and every last kid had gone home.

Too bad my teacher didn't agree.

"Well, I think you'll just have to deal with the traffic, young man, and scoot off to your next class," she said.

I thought about telling her I was paralyzed. I could fake it long enough so that she'd have to call the school nurse. The school nurse would have to come get me with a wheelchair and roll me back to the office. Then they'd call my mom to pick me up, and even though she'd probably smack the black off me when she found out I was faking, at least I'd have made it out of the school without anyone noticing what color my underwear was.

But I didn't get the chance to tell my teacher I couldn't move, because the kids in the next class were already walking in. One of them was Joey Caruso, and he was coming right toward me. "You're in my seat, dork!" he snarled, towering over me.

It was now official: I had the worst luck of any kid in Brooklyn, and maybe the world. Not only was everyone going to find out about my stupid jeans ripping open, but my archenemy would be the one who got to point it out. The only thing more horrifying that I could imagine would be if a picture of my torn pants ended up on the front page of the morning paper.

"Uh, I was just going," I stuttered.

I needed to think of something quick. Then it came to me. I could walk backward out of the classroom and into the hall. I'd lean against the wall until the bell rang and the halls were empty. Then I'd go straight to the nurse's office and she'd see what an emergency this was. Once she saw what had happened, there was no way she could make me go back to class. I didn't know all the laws, but there had to be some sort of rule against making a kid go through the school day with split pants.

I stood up very carefully.

I backed away from Joey.

I backed up all the way to the front of the room. So far, so good. I thought maybe my luck was actually changing.

I was wrong.

Some kid coming the other way bumped into me. I had to spin around to keep my balance. When I heard the roar of laughter behind me, I knew the secret was out. My underwear was staring all of them in the face. For the first time in my life, I was glad my mom always nags me to make sure I wear clean ones.

"I see London, I see France. That dork Chris split his pants!" Joey shouted. It didn't matter that it was the corniest rhyme I'd heard since third grade, it still made the other kids laugh even harder.

"That's enough," my teacher said. Apparently the class didn't agree, because they didn't stop laughing. "Chris, go to the nurse's office," she told me, trying to get control over the classroom and handing me a pass.

It was a little too late, but I was still happy to hear those words. At least I would get out of any more embarrassment. Or that's what I thought, anyway. I didn't count on the nurse making me wear my smelly gym shorts the rest of the day.

Man, Mondays just aren't my day!

Chapter 2

In my house there is only one way my mom reacts to bad news: She blames the person who tells her about it. Last year my dad was late getting home from work on Tonya's birthday because the subway he was on got stuck, and my mom *still* thought it was his fault. "You should've taken the bus!" she told him. I knew if she could blame my dad for the subways not running, she could certainly find a way to blame me for my jeans ripping. So when I walked into the house, I braced myself for my mom's famous temper.

"Chris, you're late," she hollered from the kitchen when she heard me come in.

That part *was* my fault. I took the long way home so I could avoid Jerome and his friends. Jerome is the neighborhood bully. Getting teased by Joey Caruso was bad enough; I didn't think I could handle getting teased by Jerome. Next to a bully from Bed-Stuy, Joey Caruso seems about as scary as a puppy. Jerome would definitely find a worse way to humiliate me than just changing the words to "I see London, I see France." I thought for sure that if he did catch me in those dorky shorts, he and his friends would give me a wedgie so bad that if they hung me by it from a streetlamp my feet would *still* touch the ground.

"Chris, don't act like you don't hear me," my mom shouted. "This place ain't *that* big."

I didn't answer her, because I was too distracted by Tonya and Drew. They were sitting on the sofa laughing. It wasn't the cartoons on the television they were laughing at, though, it was the baby blue gym shorts I was wearing with a button-down shirt.

"Chris, you look even sillier than that man who stands in the subway with a chicken costume on," Tonya said, giggling.

"Yeah, Chris," Drew added, covering his mouth. "Where'd you get those shorts? The lost and found?"

"Ha, ha," I said sarcastically. I'd heard so many jokes about my short shorts already, that nothing they could come up with could possibly bother me. Besides, my mom was the one I had to worry about. When she saw the hole in my jeans, she'd only think about the hole it was going to make in her wallet.

She came into the living room and took one

look at me before raising her voice. "Boy, what in the world are you wearing? I know I didn't let you go out of the house looking like a fool this morning. So what happened?"

"It's not my fault," I explained. "My pants split."

Tonya and Drew erupted in another fit. I glanced over at them and gave them the evil eye. They'd be sorry the next time I was left in charge. I'd make sure of that.

"What do you mean, your pants split? Were you horsing around again? How many times have I told you not to horse around in your school clothes? You know how much clothes cost, Chris! We can't afford you running around ripping your pants for fun!" my mom yelled.

I knew it. Somehow this was *my* fault. The way my mom acted, it was like I wanted to rip my jeans and spend all day getting teased about my lanky legs and the stink of sweat coming from those nasty shorts the nurse made me wear.

"I wasn't horsing around, I swear. They just ripped!" I shook my head. "And besides, how would I know how much clothes cost? I never get any new clothes, remember? I always get Drew's hand-me-ups, and they're already worn down when I get them. That's probably why they ripped."

My mom narrowed her eyes at me. The only thing she hates more than bad news is back talk, but there was nothing she could say this time. She knew it was the truth, so she just folded her arms and sat down. "Let me see them," she said. "I'll try to stitch them closed."

I reached into my backpack and took out what was left of my old jeans. They were almost in two halves when I handed them to my mom. She held them up and looked at the hole. Now, my mom has never thrown away a piece of clothing in her life, but even she had to admit those jeans belonged out on the curb with the rest of the garbage.

She took a deep breath and let it out real slow.

"I'll take you to get a new pair this weekend," she said.

Me, Tonya, and Drew all stared at her like her head had spun around and her eyes had popped out and fallen on the floor. I wouldn't have been surprised to find out the entire city had stopped for a second when she spoke those words. A new pair! Did I hear her right?

Then Tonya started to whine that she wanted a new pair too. Then I *knew* I'd heard right.

It was a miracle! The only time anyone in my house gets new clothes is at the beginning of the school year.

"If Chris is getting new jeans, can I get a new pair of sneakers?" Drew asked.

"Ain't no one else getting anything new!" my mom shouted. "And I don't want to hear another word about it, understand?" Then she got up and went back into the kitchen to finish cooking dinner. That meant she was done discussing it, and we all knew better than to bring it up again.

Tonya and Drew groaned, but I couldn't stop smiling. My luck was actually changing. But there was still one little thing that needed fixing. See, when you're in junior high, the only thing more embarrassing than splitting your pants in school is getting caught clothes shopping with your mom.

I followed my mom back into the kitchen. "Mom?" I asked.

"What is it?" she said as she put a meat loaf into the oven.

"Maybe I could go tomorrow after school to get new jeans," I suggested.

"Chris, you know I'm too busy to run around shopping during the week."

"Yeah I know," I said. "That's why I could go by myself."

"By yourself?" asked my mom. The way she said it made it sound like I was crazier than the guy in the commercials who screamed and yelled about how his prices for televisions were so low, they were insane.

"Why not? It's not like I'm a kid anymore," I told her. I'm thirteen, which makes me a teenager. After the age of twelve I could get a job, and I'm not allowed to eat for half price at the BBQ restaurant any longer. As far as the law is concerned, I'm not a kid. Maybe not by much, but still it's a fact. Even my mom had to admit that. "So, can I?"

I know there is such a thing as pressing your luck, but since I don't usually have any to press, I didn't think there was much to lose. So I asked her one more time to let me go shopping by myself after school the next day.

"Well, it would save me some time," my mom mumbled. "And I was supposed to get my hair done on Saturday."

"See! I could take care of this, and then you wouldn't have to give up any of your free time," I said. I tried my best to sound responsible. I could tell it was working when she smiled. She was thinking about spending all day Saturday at the beauty parlor instead of dragging me along to fight the crowds trying to find a pair of jeans that fit and were also on sale.

"I guess that makes sense," my mom admitted. "But you remember to find a pair that's a little too big. This pair needs to last, so you'd better have room to grow into them. I don't want to hear you asking for another pair a few months from now 'cause these are already too tight, understand?"

"Definitely," I said. I'd buy pants as big as a tent if it meant my mom wouldn't be waiting outside the dressing room to make sure the butt fit.

It was a victory for me. A small victory, but a victory nonetheless.

I ran up to my room to start my homework. Somehow I'd managed to turn an embarrassing situation into something positive. Things were starting to look up.

Chapter 3

"Hey, Chris, you want to hang out after school today?" Greg asked me the next day as I was getting books from my locker. Normally I would've said yes without even thinking about it. Hanging out with Greg means going to his house and playing his Atari until my hands get tired of holding the joystick.

"Not today, Greg, I can't," I told him.

"Why not? Do you have a date or something?

Does she have a friend?" Greg asked. Then he got that excited look on his face that he always gets when he thinks about girls. It makes him look sort of crazy, which is probably the reason girls don't like to talk to him.

I shook my head. "Don't you think I would've told you that?" If I ever actually get a date, Greg will be the first person I'll tell, just so he'll stop asking me if I have one.

"Then why can't you hang out?" he asked.

"I have to go and get a new pair of jeans," I told him. "Or did you forget what happened yesterday?"

Greg smiled and tried his best not to laugh. "You did look pretty funny wearing those shorts."

"Thanks," I said, rolling my eyes at him and slamming my locker shut.

As we started walking to our next class, I told Greg how my mom was letting me go by myself. "Whoa, hold up. She gave you money? Wow!" he said. Greg had been my friend long enough to know just how rare it was for my mom to trust anyone with money.

"I know, I could hardly believe it myself," I told him. Even now that I had the money, I still had a hard time believing it. I checked four times on the bus just to make sure it was still where I hid it and that I wasn't dreaming.

"Let me see it," Greg said.

"I can't. It's in my shoe," I revealed. I'd have to be crazy to keep it anywhere else. Inside your shoes is the only place a bully won't check, unless of course he wants your shoes! But my mom's hand-me-up policy includes shoes, too, so my sneakers aren't even worth stealing.

"Oh," said Greg. "That seems like a good place."

"The best," I stated with confidence. My dad's always telling me shoes are safer than the bank when it comes to hiding money. I just wished it wasn't so uncomfortable when I walked.

"How much did she give you?" he asked me. "I bet it's enough to buy Pitfall!"

"What's Pitfall?" I asked, raising my eyebrows. It sounded like some new type of danger on the subways. There were already enough creeps looking to rob me that I didn't need to start worrying about falling into giant pits every time I needed to take the train.

"What's Pitfall? It's only the best new Atari game!" Greg shouted. "I heard the graphics are amazing. It's supposed to look almost real."

"Really?" I asked in disbelief. A new video game is pretty much the most exciting thing that can happen in my life. Every time a new one comes out, it is like they invented a new holiday just for kids, and I can't wait to celebrate it.

"Really," said Greg. He always knows about

the newest games. If he spent half as much time on schoolwork as he does paying attention to video games, he probably could skip high school and go straight to college.

"Man, I wish I had that game." I sighed. In fact, I just wish I had an Atari instead of having to play video games at the arcade all the time.

Greg stopped walking and grabbed my arm. His eyes got all big and goofy-looking. They always get that way when a new plan is hatching in his head. "I know," he said. "You could use the money your mom gave you to buy the game. Then you could play it at my house whenever you wanted."

"Aren't you forgetting something?" I asked.

"What?"

"That I actually *need* a new pair of jeans," I told him. "Not to mention that my mom would kill me, and I can't play video games if I'm dead."

Greg waved his hand in the air. "Don't worry about it," he said. "I have tons of jeans. I'll give you a pair of mine, then your mom will never know."

"I don't know." It sounded like an okay plan, but I knew Greg's plans never worked out the way they were supposed to.

"What could go wrong?" he asked.

"I could get caught," I said.

I imagined my mom finding out I'd spent the money on a video game. I pictured her turning into King Kong and dragging me up the Empire State Building. Only I wouldn't be saved like the pretty lady in the movie. She'd toss me all the way back to Brooklyn, where I'd have to wear gym shorts for the rest of my life as my punishment.

"Come on, Chris, you'll be the coolest kid in school when people find out that you have the newest game out . . . and that you got it by stealing money from your own mom," Greg said. "That's hardcore."

Greg had a point. There are very few ways to gain instant coolness in our school. Having the newest video game is one. Stealing is another. Doing both at once might just make me the coolest kid at Corleone Jr. High.

"You're right, it is hardcore," I said with a smile. I could almost see the way the other kids would look at me after they found out. They'd admire me. Or at the very least, it would make them forget about me splitting my pants.

"Cool, we'll go after school and buy it," Greg said.

"It's a plan," I agreed. Then we shook hands as the warning bell rang. It wouldn't be long before we were sitting in front of his television, ruining our eyes and rotting our brains. I could hardly wait.

Chapter 4

The school day always takes longer when I know something exciting is going to happen afterward. It's like time goes by in slow motion. But eventually the last bell rang, and I rushed to meet Greg at his locker.

"You ready?" I asked.

Greg shoved some books in his locker and took others out. Then he slammed it closed. "Ready!" he announced.

The video game store wasn't far from our school. Greg and I ran the whole way there. I was worried they'd sell out of games before we got there. If the game was as good as Greg said it was, I imagined every kid in Brooklyn was going to want one.

When we walked in, I was relieved to see the guys who worked at the store playing Pitfall. We watched them for a few minutes to make sure it was really worth the risk I was taking. It didn't take long for me to figure out that it most certainly was.

"Man, look at those graphics!" I marveled. I could actually tell the guy in the game was a person. In most of the games, the people just look like boxes with arms and a smaller box for the head.

"Yeah, it looks so real," Greg said. "Especially that log."

I took a closer look. "I think that's an

alligator," I said when the log opened its mouth.

"Whatever," said Greg. "It still looks amazing."

I couldn't argue with that. The one thing I *could* argue with was the price. When I asked the guy how much it was, I was shocked. The game cost two dollars more than my mom had given me for a pair of jeans. And that was before tax! I'd have to use some of my own money from my part-time job at the corner store. This was turning out to be a pretty expensive gamble.

"You kids want to buy it or not?" the clerk asked.

"I don't know," I mumbled. Then I turned to Greg. "That's a lot of money."

But Greg wasn't about to let me leave that store without the game. "I'll chip in the extra amount," he offered. "Then it won't cost you anything, just what your mom gave you."

That seemed fair, but I still wasn't sure. I was starting to have second thoughts about the whole plan. After all, my mom had trusted me with more money than she'd ever trusted any of us with before. If I blew this, she'd never trust me again. I'd have to go clothes shopping with her for the rest of my life.

"Kid, trust me, it's worth it," the guy behind the counter said. "This game has ninety-nine levels! Then after that, you can go through the boards backward."

My jaw dropped open. Ninety-nine levels seemed impossible. It would take us weeks to finish the game. And then, if we could go backward through the boards, that doubled it. I did the math in my head, and it turned out that buying the game was cheaper than playing one arcade game a day for the same amount of time. It was a good deal.

"All right, I'll take it," I said.

"You won't regret it, kid," said the clerk. I sure hoped he was right.

I took the money out of my shoe as he put the game into a bag. The money was a little wet and smelled like cheese, but he didn't seem to mind. Even if he did, I don't think Greg or I would've noticed. We were too excited to care about anything but playing Pitfall.

As soon as we got outside, we took the game out of the bag. We must have read the back of the box twenty times. I was happy just holding it. There was a treasure chest on the box, and it felt like I'd found some buried treasure myself.

"Let's go try it out," Greg suggested.

"You bet!" I said.

We ran all the way back to his house. When we got there, we tore the game open like it was Christmas morning and turned it on. Up close, it was even better than it had looked at the store. It was almost better than Space Invaders, and that is my favorite game ever.

Greg and I took turns trying to beat each level. There was a different trick to each one, and it took some figuring out at first. I can't understand why parents think video games are such a waste of time—it takes some serious thinking to figure out these boards. It takes more thinking than most of my homework, anyway.

I was having so much fun that I lost track of time. It wasn't until Greg's mom told him it was almost time for dinner that I realized I needed to get going. I handed the joystick to Greg and told him I had to leave.

"See you tomorrow," Greg said without taking his eyes off the TV.

"Do you think you could get me a pair of your jeans before I go?" I reminded him.

"Oh, yeah," he said, pausing the game. Then he rushed over to his closet and dug out a pair of jeans from the bottom. "Here you go," he said, tossing them at me before rushing back to play the game.

I held the jeans up. They looked a little small, but I didn't have time to try them on. I was already late, and my house was two bus rides away. Besides, Greg was about the same size as me, give or take. I shoved the jeans into the plastic bag that came with the game, so it would look like they came from a store. Then I hurried out to catch the next bus. It looked like our plan was going to work to perfection.

Chapter 5

My mom held up the jeans and looked them over. My mom takes buying clothes about as seriously as buying a car or a house. She looked over every inch of those jeans so closely I was surprised she didn't call in an inspector for a second opinion! She looked at the front of the pants, and then the back. Then she spun them around and looked at the front again. She tested the button and the zipper and examined the seams. I saw wrinkles of doubt creep onto her forehead as she closed one eye and held the jeans at arm's length to see how they'd look on me. "These look a little small, you sure they fit?" she asked. I thought for sure she was onto me.

"Yeah, I'm sure," I lied. For the first time in my life, I found myself wishing Tonya would rush into the room whining about something. Anything. If I could only keep a straight face until something else distracted my mom, then I'd get away with it.

"You tried them on?" my mom asked suspiciously.

"Of course I tried them on," I told her, though I could tell just by looking at them that they were probably too small. I figured maybe they would stretch once I wore them. I really hoped she didn't ask me to try them on before then.

"Chris, I told you to make sure you bought

these bigger so you could grow into them," my mom said, shaking her head the way she does to let any of us kids know she's disappointed by something we've done.

"I did! They'll be fine," I assured her. "That's the new style." I tried to sound convincing and walked over to take the jeans from her before she had the chance to ask any more questions.

"Style? Boy, you know I don't care about no new style. I only care about the cost. I thought letting you go alone was a mistake," she said. Then she asked if there was any change, and I shook my head. "Now I *know* it was!"

I could feel my stomach getting funny when she closed one eye and got that serious look on her face that meant she thought there was something strange going on. I had to get out of that room before she decided to make me return them for another pair. I'd never get to play Pitfall again if that happened. That'd be a disaster! Greg and I had only made it through twenty levels. There were still seventy-nine more to see before I'd be satisfied.

At that moment Tonya came running into the room, just as I'd hoped. "Mom, Drew won't let me watch my show," she whined, and I saw my chance. As soon as my mom turned her head, I snatched the jeans and darted for the stairs.

"I'm going to do my homework," I shouted and took off. Out of sight, out of mind!

By the time my dad came home for dinner, my mom had forgotten all about the jeans. She didn't bring them up even once. I sat through the entire meal with a smile on my face. I'd pulled off the switcheroo and gotten away with it. My luck was really changing!

But by the next morning, I wasn't smiling anymore. In fact, when I slipped into those jeans, I wasn't even breathing! They wrapped around me tighter than one of Joey Caruso's headlocks. Plus, they didn't even go all the way down to my ankles. It was like wearing ballerina tights made out of denim.

I can't wear these, I said to myself. They were worse than those blue gym shorts.

I shoved them in the bottom drawer of my dresser and put on a different pair of pants. I headed downstairs, hoping my mom would be too busy to notice that I wasn't wearing my freshly paid-for jeans. I didn't count on it, though. Nothing slips past my mother. I've always thought she should work as a prison guard. If she did, nobody would ever be able to escape.

I walked quietly into the dining room and kept my head down. I tried my best not to look suspicious while also trying to keep anyone from seeing what I was wearing.

I was busted right away.

"Why aren't you wearing those new jeans?"

my mom asked as soon as I sat down for breakfast. Luckily, I was expecting her to ask me that and I'd thought up a great answer.

"I will," I said. "I just have to break them in. You know, like a baseball glove."

"Hmph," my mom snorted. "I swear, if those jeans are too small, I'm going to break *you* in."

I didn't say anything. I knew better. I just filled my mouth with cereal and kept my head down. It was becoming pretty clear to me that I needed to think of some kind of plan. I wasn't going to be able to keep up this lie for very long.

Chapter 6

Greg came running up to my locker. He was smiling and waving his arms to get my attention. It was easy for him to be happy—he didn't have to face my mom's fury. He was wearing a bright yellow shirt and looked like a runaway taxicab. "Chris! You're never going to believe what happened," he shouted.

"You gave me a pair of jeans from third grade; that's what happened," I said.

"Huh?" Greg asked.

"Never mind," I said. He never got any of my jokes. "I just need a different pair of jeans, that's all. The ones you gave me are too small."

"Oh, forget about that for now," Greg said, shrugging his shoulders. That was easy for him to say. His mom wasn't the one who was going to turn into King Kong and launch him halfway across the city! But Greg wasn't paying attention to me. He was too focused on what it was he wanted to tell me. "You got to hear about this one part in the game!" he exclaimed.

I listened to Greg tell me about the one board. He was so excited I thought he was going to split *his* pants with excitement. It had something to do with quicksand and cobras, but I couldn't really picture it. Mostly because I was too busy thinking about my pants problem. If Greg didn't have another pair, I was going to have to figure something else out.

There's one person who always pops into my mind whenever I need to get ahold of something that I don't really have the money for. That's Risky. He lives in my neighborhood and always sells things for much cheaper than any store. Of course, he doesn't always have *exactly* what you need. For instance, if I wanted a pair of parachute pants, he'd probably have a pair made from a real parachute. But it would cost only a couple of dollars instead of fifty like the ones in the store. That's okay when it's my money, but not when my mom is involved. She would never stand for me wasting her money. I could just see going to Risky for a pair of jeans and coming home with a pair of orange bell-bottoms. It was never going to work.

I was ready to give up.

"Look, Greg," I said. "Maybe we should just take the game back."

"Are you crazy?" he asked.

"Man, I was crazy to listen to your plan in the first place," I said. I never should've done it, and now it was time to get out of it before I got into trouble. At least, that's how I felt until Jennifer came up to my locker and smiled at me.

Jennifer is the baddest girl in our school. I hear even some of the teachers are afraid of her. She gets detention so many times it's printed on her class schedule. But besides being the girl who gets into the most trouble, Jennifer is also one of the prettiest girls in school.

"Hey, Chris," she said, and my heart skipped a beat. Jennifer only talked to boys who were as bad as she was. I didn't think she even knew my name. I was so surprised, my mouth stopped working. I stood there stuttering like a fool.

"Hey," said Greg, but Jennifer pushed him aside and stood right next to me.

"Hi," I finally managed to squeeze out.

Jennifer moved closer to me. Any closer and

we'd have been hugging each other!

"Is it true you stole money to buy a video game?" she asked.

How did she find out? Then I glanced over at Greg and saw him look away. I couldn't believe it—he'd actually told people! I'd have been real mad at him, except it was sort of working in my favor.

Jennifer laughed. "It's okay, I won't tell on you or anything," she said. "I just thought maybe you'd let me play sometime."

The best I could do was stutter and nod. I was in shock. Jennifer didn't seem to mind, though; she just laughed and made me promise that we'd hang out soon. "Sure thing," I promised as the bell rang. I'd hang out with her even if it meant I had to hang upside down!

"Did you see that?" Greg asked me once Jennifer had walked away.

"See it? I lived it," I said with a smile. Even

the back of her head was prettier than any other girl who'd ever taken an interest in me before.

"I knew this game was special," Greg said. "And that was even before I played it."

"Yeah, speaking of which, I can't wait to play some more after school today," I told him. I was no longer worried about my pants problem. I was sure there had to be a pair somewhere in Greg's closet that would almost fit me. This game was bringing me too much good luck to return it.

"About that," Greg said, "my mom's having company today, so I'm not allowed to have any friends over."

"What? But it's my game," I protested. "Plus I need to get those pants or my mom is going to kill me."

"Tomorrow, I promise."

"I guess," I said. What else could I say? I'd just have to stall my mom for another day. I had absolutely no idea how I was going to do it, but I knew it wouldn't be easy. But now that Jennifer liked me, it was finally beginning to seem like it would be worth the effort.

Chapter 7

Every day that week Greg came into school with a different story about something cool he'd discovered while playing Pitfall. The further he got in the game, the crazier it sounded. It was really starting to annoy me, because I still hadn't been able to play the game since the first day we bought it. Greg came into school every day with a new reason why I wasn't allowed to go over to his house after school.

On Wednesday it was because his mom was having company.

On Thursday he told me he had a dentist appointment all afternoon.

Friday he told me the exterminator was coming to fumigate his house. Greg said the smell would linger all day, and it wasn't safe to sniff the fumes.

The only thing I smelled was his terrible excuses!

I'd had enough of *not* playing my game. I demanded that Greg let me come over on Saturday and let me play. "I'm sick of this," I told him. "I'm going to be there by lunchtime."

"Um . . . I won't be home," Greg said. He looked around nervously, as if he was making up a lie. "I'm going . . . uh . . . with my mom to visit my cousins. And we'll be gone the whole day, so how about Sunday?"

"You know I work on Sunday," I shouted.

I'd already told him that the first four times he invited me over on Sunday. If Greg wasn't my friend, I'd have thought he was trying to keep me away on purpose. I mean, he was my friend and I had already started thinking that. So if he hadn't been my friend, I'd have known for sure he was lying to me.

And to make things worse, he still hadn't found a pair of jeans that fit me. So not only did I spend all week dodging my mom, I didn't even get the reward of playing video games. The only thing I was getting was increasingly suspicious looks from my mom. Each day I could see a little more of King Kong in her eyes.

"I forgot you had to work," Greg said, letting his shoulders sag and trying to look disappointed. "We'll just have to do it Monday then, no big deal." He started to walk toward his classroom.

I wasn't going to let him off the hook that easy.

I ran up behind him. "No big deal!" I yelled. "Maybe not for you, but I'm the one who's getting nothing out of this arrangement."

Greg kept his mouth shut. I'd figured he'd at least try to say something in his defense, but he just pointed over my shoulder. But I wasn't falling for that trick again. He'd pulled the same thing two days before at the end of the day. I was about to follow him back to his house to see if maybe there was time for one quick game before his mom's company came over, when he distracted me by pointing. By the time I realized there was nothing there, he was gone. The next day he tried to claim that I'd imagined the whole thing.

Well, not this time.

It didn't matter how much Greg pointed and nodded his head, I wasn't turning around until he agreed to let me play *my* game. "You either let me over there, or I want the game back on

Monday," I insisted. "It's up to you."

"Behind you," whispered Greg.

I realized he wasn't trying to trick me the moment Joey shoved me in the back.

"Look who it is," Joey said to his friends. They were as mean as Joey, and they did whatever he told them to. "Let's see if we can make him split his pants again." Joey laughed, punching his fist into the palm of his other hand.

I threw my hands up in the air. Friday was shaping up to be as bad as any Monday. "Man, why do you always have to pick on me?" I asked.

"Because it's fun," said Joey.

He sure had a strange idea of fun! Fun to me was the roller coaster on Coney Island, arcade games, and riding my bike. Beating up on people didn't fit anywhere on my list of fun things to do.

"But if you give me that new game I heard

you got, I might just let you go this time," Joey threatened.

So that's what this was about! He wanted my game. That was the thing about bullies, they always wanted whatever you had. It didn't matter to Joey that he didn't have an Atari to play the game on. He just couldn't stand the thought of me having something he didn't.

I took a deep breath and rolled my eyes.

This game was causing more trouble than it was worth.

"I don't even have the game," I explained to Joey. Then I looked over at Greg, but he was gone. That kid is better than anyone I've ever met at slipping away whenever there's trouble. He's so good at it, sometimes I think he has special invisible powers. "I can't give you something I don't have."

Trying to reason with Joey was like trying to reason with a rock or a tree. I could talk until

I was blue in the face, and when I was done it wouldn't change a thing.

"That's too bad for you, then," Joey snapped, punching his hand harder. "I hope you brought your gym shorts today."

There was nothing more I could do except close my eyes and cross my fingers. It was a good thing I'd asked my mom to wash those gym shorts, so at least I wouldn't smell like I did on Monday. Then I braced myself for Joey's fists, but they never touched me.

When I peeked to see what was going on, I saw Jennifer standing between me and Joey. "Joey Caruso, why don't you beat it before you get hurt?" she said. Then she poked him really hard in the chest.

"Hey, I don't fight girls," Joey cried, throwing his hands up in the air.

"That's because you know you'd lose if you fought me," said Jennifer. I couldn't believe it.

I mean, I knew Jennifer was tough, but I didn't know she was tough enough to stand up to the school bully. And that wasn't even the most surprising part about it. The incredible thing was that Joey actually backed down!

I watched in amazement as he and his pals headed off down the hall. I didn't even care if it got out that I needed a girl to fight my fights. Everyone knew it was better to have a girl fight for you than it was to get beat up, especially if it meant not having to go through the day in short gym shorts. I'd even let Tonya fight for me if I knew the other person would back down and it would save me from another dose of embarrassment.

"Thanks," I said. "That was really cool of you."

Jennifer turned toward me. Then she gave me a little push into the locker behind me. "There's no way I'm letting that creep move in on my game time," she growled. "You just keep your promise, got it?"

"Got it," I said, a little surprised. As she left, I wasn't sure if she wanted to be my new girlfriend or my new bully. The only thing I knew for sure was that this whole mess was getting out of control. I needed to start cleaning it up or I was going to be in it up to my eyeballs.

Chapter 8

Just like I'd had enough of not being able to play Atari at Greg's house, my mom had had enough of me not wearing the brand-new jeans I'd bought with her money. I spent the whole weekend trying to avoid her, because every time I saw her, she asked me about them. Since I was running out of excuses, I ran out of the room anytime she came in. But like always, my luck ran out on Monday morning.

I came downstairs wearing an old pair of jeans and hoped nobody would notice. But Tonya had been watching me squirm around the topic for the last six days and finally saw her opportunity to get me in trouble. "Mom, how come Chris got a new pair of jeans and he never even wears them?" she asked. "If you let me get a new outfit, I promise I'd wear it every time it was clean."

I snapped my head around and gave Tonya a mean look.

"Would you be quiet?" I barked.

"No, I won't be quiet," shouted Tonya. "Anyway, it's the truth."

"Shhhh!" I said, trying to get her to keep her voice down. But it was too late. The damage had already been done. She'd gotten my mom's attention.

My mom gave me a long, hard look. "Where *are* those jeans?" she asked.

"They're in my room," I said. "I'm still breaking them in."

"Boy, I know you don't think I'm about to believe that," she replied. "You march right upstairs and put them on this minute, or else."

I searched my brain for one more good excuse, but I couldn't come up with one. So I pushed my chair away from the table and got up. I went up the stairs as slowly as possible. I thought that if I took long enough, I might be in danger of missing my bus. Then my mom would tell me to forget the whole thing. It was worth a shot.

I sat down on my bed and watched the clock. I wished there was some way I could make it tick faster. I kept watching it until I heard my mom walk up the first few steps. "CHRIS, HURRY IT UP! YOU DON'T HAVE ALL DAY!" she shouted.

There went my plan.

I was out of options. I went over to my dresser, pulled Greg's jeans from the bottom drawer, and put them on. They were so small I couldn't even button them closed. I could barely even walk as I headed down the stairs. They were so tight that when Tonya and Drew started laughing at me, I couldn't even take a deep enough breath to yell at them to mind their own business.

My mom wasn't laughing at all. She looked even madder than the time she found out I'd been hiding a dog in my room for two days when I was in fifth grade. In her mind, hiding those jeans was worse, because she'd actually paid for them.

"I knew those pants were too small the second I saw them," she snapped at me. "Now I know you're not going to try and tell me you tried those on."

I put my head down and admitted that I'd

never tried them on. I figured it was better than admitting that I'd used the money to buy a video game. As far as my mom is concerned, liars and thieves are just about the worst things a person can be. And being a thief is a little worse than being a liar, so I admitted to the lesser of two evils. That's what the courts call a plea bargain.

"Busted!" Drew laughed. There's nothing quite as rewarding as watching a sibling get in trouble and knowing there's no way they can drag you down with them.

My mom just stood there and shook her head. "I swear, Chris, I don't know what's the matter with you sometimes," she said. "How many times did I remind you to try them on first? I asked you to do one simple thing and you can't get that right."

"I'm sorry," I mumbled. "I'll take them back today and get another pair."

"Oh, no you won't," my mom said sharply.

"But I have to," I said. "I can't wear these."

"I know you can't," my mom agreed. "They're going back all right, but I'm not trusting *you* to do it. Now I have to give up my lunch break to take care of it, since you obviously can't do it yourself."

I couldn't let that happen! If she walked into a store with those jeans, she'd find out that I'd never really bought them. I had to handle this on my own. "I can take care of it," I pleaded. "Just give me a chance."

"You had your chance," my mom declared. "Now get me the receipt so I can get the right size."

"Receipt?" I didn't really mean to say it out loud, it just caught me by surprise.

"Yeah, Chris, the receipt," my mom answered. "You did at least remember to get a receipt, right?"

"Um, yeah," I said. "Of course I got a receipt. I'm not stupid."

"Yeah, you are, if you thought those jeans were going to fit you," Tonya put in.

"Be quiet," I said.

"You be quiet," she shouted back.

"*Both* of you be quiet," my mom ordered. "I'm not in the mood to listen to you fight." Then she complained again about having to run to the store and return the jeans. It's not that my mom is lazy. In fact, I never see her rest except when she's sleeping. That's why her lunch break is so important to her. It's the only time during the day that she has completely to herself.

I knew I could use that to my advantage. I offered one more time to exchange the jeans myself. When my mom refused, I still had one more trick up my sleeve. "Why don't we go this weekend?" I suggested. "I could go with you, and that way we could make sure they fit right."

My mom thought about it. Even if she was disappointed in me, she had to admit that it made sense. "All right," she agreed. "We'll go on Saturday. Now run back upstairs and put on something else before you're late for school."

I could barely keep from smiling as I rushed out of the room. I'd bought myself some time, and I was sure I'd be able to get out of this mess before my mom ever found out what I'd really done.

Chapter 9

I had two choices. I could try to get another pair of jeans from Greg or I could take the game back, return it, and buy a new pair. Since I'd already tried to get Greg to help me last week without success, I decided to do what I should have done in the first place. I was going to bring the game back to the store and use the money to buy jeans.

It was the perfect plan. I'd stay out of trouble

and prove to my mom that I was responsible at the same time. I thought I might even be able to break my unlucky Monday streak if I could get everything back on track. Of course there would still be the question of what I would tell Jennifer the next time she came up to me. I'd just have to deal with her at another time. I knew breaking my promise to her would cost me, but that was okay with me. Nothing she could do to me would even compare to what my mom would do if she found out the truth.

I didn't wait for Greg to find me. I went straight to his locker when I got to school. When he saw me coming, he tried to duck away. I didn't know what his problem was lately, and I didn't really care so long as I got my hands on that game.

"Wait up," I shouted. Greg ignored me and headed straight for the bathroom. I caught up to him and grabbed his sleeve before he could get inside. A few kids stopped to watch, thinking we were about to fight. They were wasting their time. It didn't matter how annoyed I was, I'd never fight my best friend.

But I would gladly give him a hard time!

"What's your deal? You've been avoiding me all week!" I said.

Greg shrugged his shoulders and gave me a goofy sort of smile. "Have I? I didn't notice."

"Man, don't give me that!" I didn't care what his reasons were for lying to me. I was done playing. "Look, I need that Pitfall game back."

"Why?" Greg asked.

"What does it matter? It's mine."

"Technically, I paid for three dollars of it," he said.

"Yeah, and I think you got your money's worth," I told him. "I've only played it once, but you've been playing it nonstop since we got it."

That's when Greg shrank away from me. "About that, there's one little thing I need to tell you." I could tell by the tone of his voice that the one little thing was going to turn into one giant nightmare for me. "See, the reason you couldn't come over last week to play Pitfall was because there's no Pitfall game for you to play."

"What's that supposed to mean?" I asked. I hoped it meant that he got grounded and his mom took the game away. That at least meant he was going to get it back at some point. But since it was Monday, I somehow doubted it would be that simple.

"It means, I sort of melted the game," Greg said.

"You WHAT?" I yelled.

"I melted it," Greg repeated.

"I heard you," I said. "I just don't understand how you could melt a game."

"It was pretty easy," Greg explained. "That second night, I played so long that I fell asleep with the game still on. It got so hot that when I woke up, the inside was all melted. I haven't been able to get it to work since."

Melted! I couldn't believe it! I'd never heard of a video game melting before.

"What about all those things you told me you found in the game?" I asked.

"I made them up. I thought you'd be mad if you knew," he admitted.

"I AM!" I yelled. I was furious.

"That's why I didn't tell you," Greg said.

I buried my face in my hands. Something like this could only happen to me. My whole plan was ruined. I couldn't take the game back if it was melted. And if I couldn't take the game back, then I couldn't get my mom's money back either. No money meant no new jeans and no way out of the jam I was in. I might as well have just left school right then, climbed up to the top of the Empire State Building, and waited there for my mom to send my behind soaring over Brooklyn.

"Man, what am I going to do?" I asked Greg.

"Look, this is all my fault. I'll pay you back all the money you spent," Greg said. For a brief moment, I thought my problem had been suddenly solved. "As soon as I get three weeks' worth of allowance," he added. I went right back to being miserable.

I didn't have three weeks to wait.

"I only have four days!" I told him.

"I'm really sorry, Chris," Greg said.

I told him it was okay. I wasn't really mad at him. It wasn't his fault, it was mine. I should have known better. I never get away with anything! I racked my brain to come up with another solution. Maybe I could ask my boss,

Doc, to give me an advance on my pay. I didn't think he actually would. Doc was cheaper than the fake Adidas people sold on Fulton Street. Still, it couldn't hurt to ask.

"Come on, we better get to class," I said. "With my luck, we'll get detention on top of everything else."

"Or worse," Greg reminded me. "Jennifer could find out you're going to break your promise. Then she'd probably break your neck."

Oh, great! I'd almost forgotten about that.

"What else could go wrong?" I asked. I saw that Greg was thinking about the question, so I stopped him. "Never mind! I don't want to know." I just wanted to make it through the day without any more bad luck. I already had all I could handle for one day.

Chapter 10

It turned out I was right about Doc. He was too cheap to advance me even a nickel. In fact, he said if I ever asked him for an advance again, I'd lose my job! I guess that thing about it not hurting to ask doesn't really apply when it comes to money.

Greg's closet wasn't any help either. I went over to his house on Friday after school and we dug out every pair of jeans we could find. Finding them wasn't easy, either. Greg's closet was messier than Times Square after New Year's Eve. It took us more than an hour just to get everything out of there. Then it took another hour to try on every pair of jeans we found.

"This is no use," I told Greg. "I think these are getting smaller the deeper we dig." The last pair I tried on barely came down to my calves, and I wouldn't have been able to zip them closed even if I used a pair of pliers.

"You're too tall, that's the problem," Greg said. "Maybe if you walked hunched over, they might look like they fit better." Then he bent his knees and lurched around his room to show me what he meant.

"That's the dumbest thing I ever heard," I told him. "Walking like that isn't going to make it any easier to zip them shut. And even if it did, am I supposed to walk like that the rest of my life?"

79

"No, just until your mom forgets about this," he replied.

Greg doesn't know my mom too well. If he did, he'd never have said that. "When it comes to buying things, my mom *never* forgets," I said. That was the truth! She never forgot about the time five years ago when I bought a candy bar with the money left over from buying milk. Now, every time she sends me to the store to pick up milk, she still reminds me not to spend the change on candy. She'll *still* be telling me that five years from now too. That's just how my mother is. And that candy bar only cost a quarter, so I could only imagine how the price of a pair of jeans was going to change my life.

"What are you going to do?" asked Greg.

The truth was that I didn't have a clue. This was my last chance at trying to stay out of trouble. We'd tried everything else I could think of. We tried to exchange Greg's jeans, but no store would take them back since we didn't have a receipt. They could also tell the jeans weren't new. One place even accused us of stealing jeans, and we had to run out of there before they called the cops.

I'd tried to borrow money too. Not just from Doc. I also tried to borrow it from Drew. He always has a few dollars hidden away. I never know where he gets it from, but he always has it. Only Drew wouldn't lend me the money because he said he was saving it for a new pair of sneakers. I explained to him that I'd pay him back in two weeks, but he was still mad at me because Mom bought my jeans but not his shoes. I couldn't exactly tell him the truth about that, either.

I even tried to earn extra money by offering to do other kids' homework. But since everybody had seen me hanging around with Jennifer, no one thought they could trust me anymore. The only thing I hadn't tried was panhandling. But with my luck, someone from my neighborhood would see and it'd get back to my mom. Acting poor fell just below lying and stealing in my mom's book. If she caught me doing that on top of the other two, she'd ground me for so long that I'd never see the light of day again.

"I guess I'm going to have to tell my mom the truth," I said. "Unless I find a bunch of money in the middle of the street, it's my only option."

"Good luck with that." Greg rolled his eyes. "I guess I'll see you next year when you're done being grounded."

"Thanks for your support," I said sarcastically.

Before I left his house, Greg gave me his allowance for that week. It was the first part of the money for the game. "I thought this might help," he said. "You know, if you had some money, maybe it might make your mom a little less mad."

"Maybe." I didn't know if that was true, but I thanked him anyway. Even though he was the one who melted the game and got me in this situation, it was still pretty nice of him to try to help me out of it. It was because of things like that that I had a hard time staying mad at Greg, no matter how rotten of a thing he'd done.

I got on the bus that would take me back to my house and to my doom. That's when I saw a pair of gloves sitting on an empty seat next to me. I also saw an umbrella rolling around under the seat in front of me. Neither of them had an owner. It gave me an idea.

Things got lost in the city all the time. The subways, the buses, and even the sidewalks were littered with things that had gotten dropped or forgotten. So I thought, if everyone else could lose stuff, why couldn't I?

I would tell my mom I'd lost the receipt, and she'd have to believe me. Sure, I'd still get in trouble. A lot of trouble! But getting in trouble for being dumb was a lot better than getting in trouble for lying and stealing.

By the time I got home, I had it all figured out. I walked up the front stairs slowly. I checked my reflection in the glass window and made sure I looked as miserable as I could. I made my shoulders sag and my mouth droop. Perfect! I was one sorry-looking sight.

My mom and dad were both waiting for me in the living room. I'd never called them to say I was going to be late, so they were already in a bad mood. "Chris, where have you been? You know you're supposed to ask us before you run off after school," my dad began.

"I know," I said quietly. I had to keep up my miserable act.

"Then why didn't you?" asked my mom.

I shrugged.

"Boy, what's gotten into you lately? Moping around and not using any sense?" my mom wondered. My plan was working. I was going to be able to turn everything around and make her think that I'd been acting strange because I felt guilty about losing the receipt. That way she'd see that even though I'd done something irresponsible, at least I felt bad about it. That was sure to give me some points in my favor.

"I don't know," I said. "I guess I've just been feeling bad."

"Is something wrong?" my dad asked.

"Sort of," I said. I looked up at them for the first time and put on an extra-miserable-looking face before going into my made-up story. "It's about the jeans I bought. You see, the reason I've been acting so funny about it is because I don't have a receipt. I lost it."

"You what?" my mom snapped. "Ain't

no store going to take back jeans without a receipt."

"I know, that's why I feel so bad about it," I told her.

For a second, I thought I saw steam come out of my mom's ears. My dad wasn't much better either. There's nothing my dad hates more than wasting money. He counts every penny that's spent and is always looking for ways to save. "Chris, you know money doesn't grow on trees," he said. "You ever see money growing on trees?"

I shook my head.

"Because it don't!" my dad stated. "I thought you'd know better, now that you have a job."

"Speaking of jobs, you're going to pay me back every cent from your paycheck," my mom informed me. That was fine with me, since Greg was paying me every cent from his allowance. It wasn't going to cost me a thing.

"I will," I said, trying to make it sound like a big burden.

"Darn right you will," my mom said. "And you also better save up, because the next pair of jeans you want, you're going to pay for with your own money. Now go get me those jeans. Maybe I can make a skirt for Tonya or something."

"Okay," I said.

"And another thing," my dad added. "You're grounded for one week."

I pretended to be upset, but really I was hiding my smile until I was out of the room. Little did they know I'd gotten off easy compared to what would've happened if they'd known what I'd really done.

I was actually pretty proud of myself. I was one smooth operator.

Chapter 11

Even though I was grounded, the weekend didn't turn out so bad. It was nice not to have anything to worry about anymore. That was the one good thing about getting in trouble—at least the problem was solved. And besides, part of my punishment was to play a game of Monopoly with Drew and Tonya. My dad thought it would teach us an important lesson about money. I wasn't sure about that, but it certainly was a nice break from the chores they had me doing all weekend.

We were playing the game on Sunday evening, and it ended up being a lot of fun. Even my mom was in a better mood. She was busy making Greg's old jeans into a skirt for Tonya, which meant Tonya was also in a good mood, so she didn't even whine when she was losing the game.

Life was good. That is, until there was a knock on our front door.

"Chris, will you answer that for me?" my mom said.

"Sure thing," I answered. I was trying my best to be helpful and get back on my mom's good side. I got up from the table and walked over to the front door. I looked through the peephole and saw Greg standing on our stoop. I didn't expect to see him there. Greg never came around my neighborhood. I knew it had to be something important.

I opened the door and he burst into the hall-way.

"Hey, Chris, I got great news!" he shouted.

His shouting brought my mom into the doorway, but Greg didn't notice. "I got my dad to take me to the video game store yesterday," he blurted out. I shook my head, hinting to him not to say anything more. I didn't know where he was going with this, but I had a feeling it was going to get me into trouble.

"Not now," I whispered.

"But this is great news!" Greg shouted even louder than before. "My dad marched in there and told them that game was defective. He made such a stink that they gave us a brand-new one."

"That's great," I said, keeping an eye on my mom to see if she was still listening. She was, and she didn't look happy. "Look, Greg, I'm kind of grounded, so maybe we could talk about this in school."

"That's what I'm trying to tell you," Greg persisted. "You don't have to be grounded anymore. Not only did my dad get them to replace the game, he also got them to give us your money back!"

Playing dumb was my only defense.

"What money?" I asked. I hoped Greg would finally figure it out.

That was giving him too much credit.

"What money? The money you were supposed to buy jeans with!" Greg laughed. Sometimes it amazes me how he can do well in school but be so dense when it comes to common sense.

I threw my hands up in the air. I couldn't believe it! My best friend had just ratted me out.

"CHRIS! GET IN HERE!" my mom yelled from the doorway. The image of King Kong popped into my head again, and it wasn't pretty.

I was in so much trouble I'd have changed places with anyone at that moment.

"Oops!" Greg said. "Um . . . here's your money."

"Yeah, thanks," I said, taking the money.

"I'd better get going," he mumbled. He took a step toward the door, then stopped. "Oh, I almost forgot. I ran into Jennifer on the way home from the store. She wasn't too happy. She gave me this to give to you." Greg reached into his pocket and took out a folded piece of paper.

I read the note. It said, "You lied! On Monday, you're dead!" I knew what that meant; I had a new bully. Jennifer would make sure to finish off whatever was left of me after my mom was done. It looked like my terrible string of bad Mondays was going to continue for another week. And now it had even spilled over to Sundays.

"See you tomorrow," said Greg. Then he went off to go play Pitfall, while I went to the living room to face King Kong.

"CHRIS!" my mom yelled from the kitchen again.

I guess what grown-ups always say about video games is actually true: They really are bad for my health!

everybody hates chris™

If you liked
Everybody Hates Best Friends,
be on the lookout for book #5,
Everybody Hates School Presentations,
coming to stores near you!

As part of Corleone Jr. High's annual acknowledgment of Black History Month, Chris's history teacher is giving extra credit to anyone who comes to school armed with "Black Facts." Chris is quickly designated the resident expert on all things African American. Then the principal decides that Chris will give a presentation—in front of the whole school—about African-American history. As if this isn't nerve-wracking enough, Chris has to work with his nemesis, Joey Caruso, on the project! Will Chris survive Black History Month?